Santa's Sack

NICOLE PARKER &
UNFORTUNATE READS

Blurb

Last year, disaster struck when Santa Claus was kidnapped and taken to Halloweenville. This year, the Seasonal Symposium Officials are putting protective measures in place.

Except...

Santa and his captor, Sackman, inadvertently discovered they shared dark carnal proclivities. They will do whatever it takes to ensure a repeat performance this year, but will just one night be enough?

No one expects Santa to beg to be on the naughty list.

Santa's Sack is a parody (sentient object adjacent) romance intended for audiences over 18 years old. This story contains intimate relations between a sack/man and Santa. Check interior content considerations for a full list of information, and read at your own risk!

To Nicole's husband, who insisted we add one more page to the ebook so it was 69 pages.

Also, sorry to Mr. Unfortunate Reads for ruining his favorite movie.

Content Considerations

The following sentient object romance story is a work of fiction and is classified as parody. If you saw the cover of this book and still picked it up, you should know it's about to get real weird, but we're going to warn you anyway.

This is a story about a Sack-person and Santa Claus having intimate relations. Some content included you should consider before reading includes kidnapping, d0m/sub dynamic, honorifics, 0ral s-x, @nal s-x, edging, bedroom accessories including candy c-rings, nipple clamps, candy flogger (which obviously also means impact play), and a St. Andrew's Cross, degradati0n, crawling, unprotected s-x, cream pie resulting from said unprotected s-x, a huge lollic0ck, glitter c-m, boring meetings because Nicole is obsessed with them for some reason but it's okay because she writes them so well, TEAMS messaging (but not the kind you think), enemies to lovers, forbidden relationship, opposites attract, s-xual awakening, exhibitionism, gummy worm filling (this will make sense later we promise), gross snake tongue, Sack Daddy, flavored spooge, and an epilogue with a leather mommy elf Domme and her two consensual subs, b0ndage, and stilettos.

Contents

Prologue

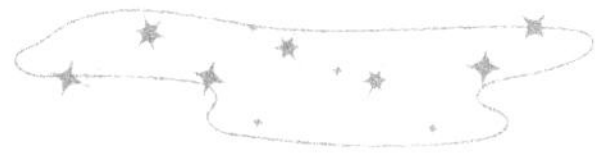

Santa

Darkness surrounds me as I come to my senses, awkwardly bound and stuffed in some kind of bag. The irony of being carted away in a sack is not lost on me, but where mine is made of a plush smooth velvet, this horrible material scratches at each jostle. Struggling against my captors proves futile, despite my best efforts. The bag is tied too securely, not even a sliver of light filtering through so I'm left trapped in the dark, attempting to cry out around the horrible smelling rags shoved in my mouth.

"Shit, he's awake," says a shrill voice.

It couldn't be one of my elves. They have no reason to betray me like this. I strive to ensure all my workers are well taken care of. Plus that voice— tinny and discordant, nothing like the sweet harmonious tones of my half-sized helpers.

My kidnappers continue on their way, jerking me around carelessly. I need to figure out who they are and why they've taken me. Providing presents to boys and girls doesn't garner you many enemies, but I've given my fair share of coal to those on the naughty list. Still, none of them should've been able to reach me in Christmastown. The barrier is closed this time of year.

I rack my brain, thinking about the conditions of my home. Things have been perfect in Christmastown. Every day is Christmas, for goodness' sake! Who wouldn't want that? Merriment. Cheer. Never-ending caroling. I shudder involuntarily at the thought - alright, maybe there are some imperfections, but it's largely what I dreamed it would be. Sure, certain aspects have become more *tediously repetitious* than initially anticipated, but a little monotony is worth it to achieve this level of happiness for everyone! Even if, on some rare occasions, I do feel like jamming a candy cane through my skull.

The unpleasant bumping and jostling finally stops and I'm dumped from the sack, falling face forward, unceremoniously sprawled in front of a large sack of a man. Blinking, my gaze travels upward as my eyes adjust to the dim light. I cringe as gummy worms slither out from unsightly stitching gaps in his body. Continuing my upward perusal, I take in his bulbous form. His snake-like tongue peeks out, wetting his lips.

His grotesque mouth curves into a wicked grin. "Well, well, well. What do we have here?"

Put Me on the Naughty List

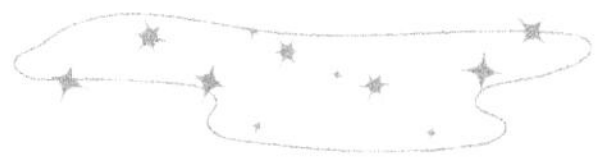

Santa

Drenched in sweat, I wrap my hand around my icicle-hard cock. I've been awake only thirty seconds and already I'm aching like an elf for cocoa, thinking of Sackman. I can distract my mind with work during the day, remaining helpless as he haunts my dreams. It's been months since the incident, but I think of him constantly.

Today I will finally see him again.

I give one slow stroke as I remember being strapped down, like a spruce to the roof of a sedan, completely at his mercy. *Stroke.* What should've been the worst night of my life instead has become my go-to inspiration when trimming my tree. *Stroke.* The twisted mix of pain and pleasure. *Stroke.* Spicy but refreshing like peppermint. *Stroke.* The way I felt completely degraded, yet completely turned on. *Stroke.* The way he used me and then discarded me, like some wadded up wrapping paper. *Stroke.* The way that no matter what I do, I can't get him out of my head. *Stroke.* I come hard, making a sparkly mess of my flannel sheets. Again.

With a groan, I roll out of bed and head toward the shower. The disaster I'm making of my sheets each morning is making it clear to the cleaning elves that I'm more than a little frustrated. No doubt word has gotten out to the other elves. Nothing stays a secret for long in Christmastown. The fact is, no one here can provide me with the particular thrill I'm seeking. Whenever I even begin to hint at what I want, my words get twisted like taffy into something sweet. But I desire something sharp: broken bulbs and barbed wire tinsel.

No one expects Santa to beg to be on the naughty list.

The faucet is set as cold as the North Pole before I step in, hoping the sudden chill will help me focus. Today is the Symposium of Seasons, the quarterly meeting of empowered seasonal representatives. It's a bunch of bureaucratic nonsense and a complete waste of time, but mandatory if you want your holiday to retain its recognition. The Springtide Snail missed just one meeting and now no one celebrates Slimy Spring Solstice. I won't risk absenteeism. Quarter after quarter we gather while someone blabbers on about holiday satisfaction scores and celebration engagement projections.

Usually I only make a point of going in winter, sending a representative for the other seasons. After the fiasco this past Christmas, though, the Occasion Official has demanded that I be in attendance myself. I didn't protest, mostly because I know Sackman will be stepping in for Halloween, replacing Calabaza, much to the board's disapproval. I will not miss an opportunity to see him, even if it means sitting through hours of agonizing agenda items.

The frigid water is not enough to completely eliminate the memory of the dream and I have to rub out one more present from my sack to prepare myself for this meeting.

Rifling through my closet, I try to find a suit that will make me look good, but not make it look like I'm trying *too* hard. My hands run over the multitude of red options. Should I consider diversifying my wardrobe? Another color? Would he prefer me in black, I wonder...

Realizing I'm going to be late, I finally pick one, grabbing a thick black belt to tie together the ensemble. Next are my leather boots and gloves, then a search for my hat before running out the door. Luckily, the meeting is only a quick fifteen-minute sleigh-ride even without using my Christmas magic. The reindeer are already harnessed as I hop into my sleigh, nudging them to pick up the pace, repeating to myself there's no special reason I'm so eager to get to this meeting.

My lead elf, Spinkletark, and I sit at the long conference table reviewing the agenda when Sackman enters the room. There's no need to look. I can feel it in my bones. Trying to remain calm, I continue perusing the screen before me, but the monster of a man consumes my thoughts. He slides about the room confidently, drawing resentful glares from other attendees before taking the seat directly across the table from me. I finally get the nerve to slyly glance up at him, just to find him obviously staring at me with those void-black eyes and a sardonic grin. It's hard to force down a swallow, my mouth suddenly dry as days-old gingerbread. My dreams have not done this beast justice. His very essence seeps malevolent intent.

Aiming for nonchalant, I reach for a glass of water, my heart thundering inside me like an arctic blizzard. The Occasion Official calls the meeting to order and begins going over old business, but my attention never wavers from Sackman's rugged burlap hands, imagining their coarse touch.

"... and I think we can all agree that after the disaster we had last Christmas..." At the mention of my holiday, my attention snaps back to the present, and I turn to face the Occasion Official only to find them glaring pointedly at Sackman.

"It's best if we limit our inter-holiday mingling to just the Symposium of Seasons. Any and all communication between holidays will be monitored by the newly appointed Celebration Scanners."

I inwardly grumble at the idea of these new prying eyes as the OO continues to drone on about how they plan to monitor our every action to prevent another holiday disaster in the future. My outward position on the matter has to at least appear supportive of this initiative. I was a victim in this matter per official accounts, but it's hard not to show my disapproval at this obvious invasion of privacy.

Initial outrage passing, my mind wanders ahead to possible complications and consequences, perhaps new dangers presented... and damn it all if the new forbidden aspect of anything with Sackman only makes it that much hotter. The possibilities mull in my head like wine, becoming sweeter and spicier until I feel a similar heat in my chest, when suddenly something slithers up my leg. Internally panicking, I attempt to shake whatever it is off my leg discreetly, but it's no use. The thing keeps creeping up under my trousers, toward my thigh. Eyes darting, they make contact with Sackman, whose smile is so wide and wicked that I know he has something to do with this. The thing crawls up to my hip, wriggling beneath my boxer briefs and making its way to my cock, where it securely squeezes itself around my length. My package has been wrapped with a wormy ribbon, and I can't help but gasp, drawing unwanted attention to my situation. Trying desperately to cover it up, I cough a few times into my handkerchief, reach down, and try to adjust things.

I look down at my computer and see a new Text Exchange Application for Merriment Symbols (TEAMS) message.

Sackman: I'll be eating that off you later.

A frisson of surprise shooting through me, he gives me a devious wink while licking his dry lips. A whimper escapes as I reach again for my water.

Sackman: Are you a gambling man, Santa?

It's a valiant attempt to ignore the message, but it doesn't take long until another comes through.

Sackman: How about we make a little wager? You make it through this ordeal of an assembly without getting caught, and your punishment won't be so severe.

I choke, spraying water on the table.

"Santa, are you alright? Is there something you wanted to say?" The OO asks, looking perturbed at my interruption.

The entire room looks at me, and I turn red as my suit, shaking my head and pretending to focus intently on my screen again.

Sackman: Well, that certainly did not take long. I guess you lose.

Santa: I never agreed to play. You cheated.

Sackman: I never said anything about playing fair.

Meeting the soulless black depths where his eyes should be, I check for a reaction. He seems completely unaffected by our conversation. The clock taunts me as I count down the minutes until this meeting ends and Sackman can come through on his threats.

I Have a Huge...

Sackman

This meeting is a nightmare, and that's saying something since I'm sorta in the business of things that go bump in the night. Ever since Calabaza–the pumpkin-headed fool–went off and got *married*–blegh–I've been in charge of Halloweenville, which is how I ended up here in this sad beige conference room listening to a bunch of merry maniacs discuss quarterly goals.

Seriously, for a meeting of the head honchos of holidays, this event is drab. These prudes need to loosen up a little. Well, I know how to get one of them to loosen up, at least.

When Santa chokes on his water, it takes all my willpower not to smirk in satisfaction. After last year's indecent incident, I don't want to draw any attention to myself, but he just makes it so easy to fuck with him.

One little gummy worm is all it took to have him on edge. Granted, that sour slitherer is now squeezing the base of his candy cane...

Inconspicuously reaching down, I readjust my semi-hard cock. I'm a little on the larger side...

You know what? I'll just say it.

I have a huge dick.

Being a big boy means big *everything*, and thinking about tasting jolly old Nicky over there is proving to make me mighty uncomfortable in my lower-sack right now.

My eyes never leave his, a battle of wills ensuing to see who breaks the connection first. It's cute that he's even trying when he knows he wants me to do all sorts of things to him that would land him on the naughty list. As expected, he tears his gaze from mine with bright red cheeks.

Hmm, those reddened cheeks remind me of the new toy I had commissioned in the off season. Last year was so unexpected, when that succulent ass jiggled with every slap of my roughened palm, the red handprints getting brighter after each round I knew I needed to up the stakes this year.

Grinning, I message Santa again.

Sackman: When this meeting ends, you know where to go. If you're a good boy and don't make me wait, I may even let you off with a lighter punishment despite you losing our bet.

No more messages are exchanged as the meeting finally wraps up. Sounds of clothing rustling and chair legs scraping against the floor fill the room as all the empowered seasonal representatives hurry to scuttle out. Well, everyone except that goodie two shoes Tina Toothfairy. She's lingering near the OO with pathetic doe eyes, just hoping he will give her a little extra attention. Some people may like that innocent act, but I prefer a little debauchery. And if I can corrupt someone good in the process? Yeah, that's my–

"Mmph." A grunt scrapes out of me when something hits my back, causing me to lean one hand on the table to avoid tipping to the ground. "What the fuc–"

"Oh gosh, Mr. Sackman sir, I am so sorry. Are you ok? Can I help you? Here, let me pick up your..."

The lean man trails off as I slowly turn around to face him. His gaze moves up, up, up until he reaches my face, taking a big gulp at what he sees there–or rather what he doesn't.

Like I said, I'm a big boy. Tall and thick, my body certainly isn't one that would end up on the cover of Seasons Illustrated, but it's the lack of eyes that always seems to freak people out. It used to bother me, but now I use it to my advantage, embracing the menacing force I was always meant to be.

This kid doesn't look away though, and I wonder if he's too stupid to realize who he's dealing with. As much as I'd like to ignore him, he's now blocking my way out. A growl rumbles up my throat before I open my mouth to speak.

"Do *not* presume to touch me, or my things. I don't even know who the hell you are."

Oh great, now he's shaking like an autumn leaf, clearly terrified but unmoving. Yep, too stupid to even run.

Finally he stammers out, "I-I-I'm Reginald, Mr. Sackman, uh...sir. I...uh...I'm..."

"Spit. it. OUT. Reginald." My voice booms throughout the now near-empty conference room. I don't have time for this.

I need to get back to my lair where a good little toy should be arriving very shortly, ready for me to unwrap and play with him.

"I'm-your-new-Celebration-Scanner!" The words whoosh out on one breath, clearly in an attempt not to draw my ire yet again.

Ah yes, the beleaguering glorified hall monitors that the Occasion Official has appointed to spy on us this year. What the board thinks they will discover with their little minions is beyond me. I personally believe it's a waste of committee funds, but no one cares what I think.

Still glaring at Reginald, I reach into my bag and pull out a card. But when I go to hand it to the little twerp, he flinches back. If I had eyes, they would be rolling so hard right now. This guy won't survive the week, much less long enough to gather any useful information. Reaching forward, I tuck the card into his breast pocket and nearly do a double-take. *Is that a fucking pocket protector?*

Eager to escape this awkward encounter, I grumble at Reginald. "Contact my assistant Cynthia. Trust me, you do *not* want to run into me again."

With that warning, I step around the still chattering pipsqueak, bag in my hand and determination in my strides.

It's time to see what I'm stuffing Santa's stocking with this year.

Fuck Gluten Free Cookies

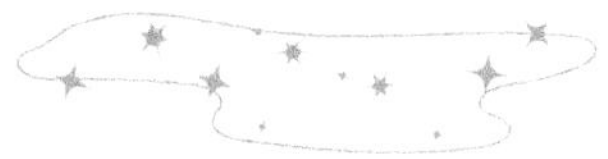

Santa

Spinkletark is blabbing on about who the fuck knows what. Perhaps if I had paid attention to anything other than the sexy sack of a man across from me at that meeting, I'd have more to contribute to the conversation. The gummy worm cock ring is pulling all my focus away from my elf companion and I know if I don't find a way to deal with this soon, we're going to have a white Christmas on our hands.

"Well, Santa? What do you think? Good idea?" When I don't respond, they misread my hesitation and continue, "Best idea?"

Fuck. This is what I get for not paying attention. Last time I agreed to one of Spinkletark's harebrained ideas, we shifted to only gluten-free cookies for a whole Christmas season. Not going down that chimney again. Fuck that nonsense.

"Santa, sir?" Turning, I find Hazel. I recognize her immediately from the nice list. She's the image of the sexy librarian fantasy come to life, but if memory serves, she's nothing more than a pencil-pushing bureaucrat. At least she'll buy me some time to figure out what the fuck Spinkletark was yapping about. She reaches out a hand to shake mine.

"Hazel Cracklebottom. Big fan of your work, sir."

"How can I help you, Ms. Cracklebottom?" I offer my cheeriest smile.

"I am the Celebration Scanner assigned to your case. I'll be relocating to Christmastown to assist by monitoring any and all communication with other seasonal sectors."

"Oh Ms. Cracklebottom, I've seen your excellent work and secured your place on the nice list for a long time. I know you mean well, but I don't think that any of that will be necessary. We've tightened up security significantly since the incident. All the elves know self defense now." Turning to Spinkletark, I ask, "Isn't that right, Spinkle?"

"Yes, of course!" They agree, raising their hands in a defensive posture.

"Oh, thank you Santa. It means a lot to me, really. I'm sure we'll find out soon enough that I'm completely redundant in Christmastown, everything being on the up and up, but until then, I will be around monitoring everything," she says with a cheery smile.

That won't do.

"Alright then. Spinkletark, why don't you take Ms. Cracklebottom here-"

"Hazel," she interrupts.

The forced smile I'm sporting probably looks more grimacy than cheery. "Yes, Ms. Hazel, back to Christmastown with you on the sleigh. There was one last thing I wanted to discuss with the OO before I left for the day. I'll find my own way home." I wave as Spinkletark leads Hazel away.

Once they're out of sight, I consider dealing with my gummy worm issue immediately. Although, I can't imagine what punishment Sackman would inflict if he found out I removed the worm myself. Would he beat me? *Degrade me?* Do something my holly jolly mind can't even conceive? The devilish worm squeezes around my cock as I harden at the thought of Sackman's depravity.

My gait is stiff as I discreetly try to adjust my trousers, making my way toward the conference room once again. If I can at least get this damnable Celebration Scanner reassigned it will be one less obstacle in my way. Turning the final corner before the conference room, I run into the man of my nightmares.

"Well well well, this isn't where you're supposed to be, jolly man," he growls, moving closer, pinning me against the wall.

"I, um," I stammer, looking up and down the hallway, my mind unclear if I am searching for help or hoping to not be seen. I don't know what it is about this man that gets me so flustered so quickly. Trying to calm myself, I swallow and take a deep breath. "I was going to ask the OO to get my Celebration Scanner reassigned."

One side of his mouth kicks up. "Ooooh, big red has a naughty streak, eh? Not such a good boy, after all, are you Santa?"

"Mr. Sackman, sir, you wouldn't be having inappropriate conversations with Mr. Santa, would you?" A small man, close to tears, has joined us in the hallway. Every ounce of his body language is screaming that he does not want to be having this conversation.

Without turning away from me, Sackman replies, "Santa, meet my Celebration Scanner, Ryan-"

"It's Reginald, sir." Reginald cowers, even as he says it.

"Not important. He was just on his way to speak with my assistant, Cynthia. Weren't you, Rupert?" He continues looming over me, so very close. We're not touching, but it wouldn't take much to close the distance.

"Reginald, sir. And sirs, I have to report on any conversations between the two of you. It's my assignment, given to me by the Occasion Official themself," Reginald squeaks out.

"It's alright, Reg. I think our business is pretty much all *wrapped up* here. Just going to *grab* something that I lent to dear old Santa Claus. Let me just *squeeze* in a minute here and our business will be concluded." With each word, the candy crawler coils tighter and tighter. Beads of sweat break out across my forehead as I hold my breath.

Reginald looks between us. I close my eyes, attempting to take deep breaths, which only results in me inhaling Sackman's musk. He smells dank and musty, but with a hint of spice. If Reginald doesn't leave soon, he's going to get a show the poor boy's not ready for, because I don't know how much longer I can hold back.

Finally, I hear the click of Reginald's heels receding down the hall and I let out a sigh of relief. That is, until I feel Sackman grab my belt.

"Here?" I whimper.

He leans in close to whisper in my ear. "You heard the little man, no more words, Claus."

Grabbing my hat, he jams the large fluffy pom-pom into my mouth, causing me to gag. He holds the tip of his hand in front of his lips and whispers, "Shh," before roughly undoing my belt and yanking down my pants.

Something to Put the Edge On

Sackman

We shouldn't be doing this in the hallway. It's risky. But I've always liked living on the edge and seeing Claus sweaty and red, knowing it was my gummy worm making him flustered, has me throwing caution to the winter wind.

Sometimes things are harder for me–heh pun totally intended–with the lack of fingers and all, but nothing can stop me from freeing Santa's rock candy-hard cock. Heat builds within me as I take in the glorious sight. It's red and swollen, my gummy worm strangling it until glittery pre-cum leaks steadily from the throbbing tip.

Even his cum is holiday themed, for Reaper's sake.

Usually I keep a tough facade, but I've been thinking about spreading that festive seed all over both of us since the incident last year, rubbing it in until we both glow with Christmas cheer.

A gasp sounds from the jolly old soul as my rough palms suddenly grip his shaft, deftly stroking his merry member. There's time to draw this out later in my lair, but this has to be fast, so we aren't caught by those pesky Celebration Scanners.

"Did my worm ring drive you crazy during that snoozefest of a meeting? You looked so bored I thought you could use a little distraction." My voice is rough in his ear.

Santa tries to say something around the gag in his mouth, but all I hear is muted mumbling. I'm tempted to leave it in but eagerness to hear what he has to say wins out, and I pull out the pompom.

As he's trying to wet his lips so he can speak, I purr, "What was that?"

"M-More like a...b-big distraction." It's nearly a whimper.

"Mmmm you like stroking my ego while I stroke this christmassy cock, don't you my slutty little snowman? Do you think that's going to get you out of your punishment?"

As my strokes speed up, his breathing becomes heavier. Reaching down to his baubles, I give them a squeeze and they tighten, letting me know he's close. Immediately ceasing my strokes, my hands instead tuck his cock back into his red velvet pants before pulling them back up over his plump ass. Santa lets out a cry of frustration that I silence with my palm.

Keeping my hand over his mouth, I send a couple of gummy worms to do up his thick black belt. Heat seeps into my skin from the flush over his entire body, the result of taking him right to the edge but not allowing him to go over. I tsk at him.

"Did you really think I was going to let you come that easily? Oh, sweet snowy child, you should know better than that. Besides, we can't let those sniveling spies catch us before we've had our real fun, can we?"

Footsteps ring down the hallway as I lean back away from his bowl full of jelly, giving his rosy cheek a couple of nice pats before I fully move away. Reginald's whiny voice gets louder as he comes closer to where we are standing in the hall.

Fuck. Why can't I get rid of this little asshole?

My mind whirrs as I consider options to dismiss the twerp yet again, but luck is on my side because before he reaches us, another Celebration Scanner stops him for a conversation. With Reggie distracted, it's time for me to get out of here.

Turning back to Santa with a sinister smirk, I say, "That was close, but I think it's time we leave, don't you? Why don't you use that silly little button nose of yours," I lean forward to boop him on the tip with my pointed hand, "and shimmer on over to my lair so we can finish what we started."

His eyes widen before he nods sagely, still panting from our encounter. Taking a step back to give him room, my eyes never leave his as he reaches his gloved hand toward his face and taps one thick finger against the side of his nose, causing a whirlwind of sparkles and magic to surround him before he poofs out of existence.

Smirking internally to myself, I shove my hands into my pockets and saunter toward the portal to Halloweenville, whistling Jingle Bells under my breath the whole way.

Not Even One Gumdrop

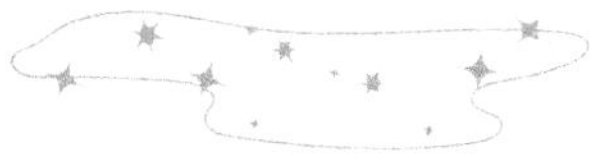

Santa

What the fuck am I doing? I look around Sackman's lair in a combination of horror and twisted lust. The last time he had me here, I was left dangling like some damnable ornament, his to gawk at. Is a Sackman ride in a nightmare land of pleasure worth risking what I have built in Christmastown? Given the 'giddy up, let's go' feeling in my pants, Santa's little helper sure seems to think so.

There's a noticeable wet spot on the front of my trousers from where that sack of sin left me in an awful predicament. That figgy gummy worm! Would Sackman like seeing the effect he has on me? Or should I find a better way to make my holiday display? *Why do I even care so much about what he thinks?*

Rubbing my beard nervously between my gloves, I take in my surroundings, trying to come up with a plan. Sackman will be here soon, assuming he is not planning to torment me further by making me wait. The portal is just a short walk from his lair on the edge of town. Even if I didn't have my magic to get me to and from places in an instant, it still wouldn't be very difficult to visit him here. Convenient location with few prying eyes, and everyone in Halloweenville knows to keep their head down, unlike Christmastown with all the prying busybodies. I wonder if he uses that to his advantage with other visitors.

Not that it concerns me one bit. Nope. Not even one gum-drop.

My gaze snags on the hook from my last visit looming above me, other familiar sights like skeletons, chains, and cages surrounding it. Sackman has added to his collection of nefarious devices since I was here last: a stretching rack, a St. Andrew's cross, and even a pillory.

A flurry of excitement like a crisp winter wind courses through me as I imagine the possibilities, but I don't want to seem overeager. I'm not some child, peeking in their stocking before Christmas morning, yet the North Pole tenting my pants isn't exactly subtle.

Putting on an air of indifference, I make my way to the large round table he strapped me to the last time. This should work nicely for my purposes. I quickly toe off my boots and shimmy out of my clothes, tossing them to the side, too excited to find a proper place to stash them. Feeling self-conscious—and a bit cold now completely nude—I retrieve and pull back on my oversized red coat and hat. He seems to enjoy my signature look, anyway.

As I crawl onto the table, my mind races trying to find the right pose to surprise him with. On my side to give him the best view of my peppermint stick? Or should I get on my hands and knees, my ample Christmas caboose on display? Perhaps lie on my stomach with my ankles crossed like an innocent schoolboy?

I'm moving to my knees when I hear him scuffle down the hall. Ass it is. I give my cock a couple of tugs, wanting to impress my giant goody bag. After his teasing in the meeting, our hallway confrontation, plus the anticipation of him finding me like this, I think the right look from him might make Christmas come early tonight.

"Like I said, Robbie-" His voice echoes down the hall as he approaches.

"Reginald, sir."

"I'm going to make some snake and Reginald stew if you don't let me get back to my work. Either speak to Cynthia or, better yet, Calabaza. He's a big softie now. I'll bet he has all the time in the world to listen to you ramble."

Fuck. Maybe I should hide? Teleport to safety? I'm reaching my hand to my nose when I notice my pants, shoes, and dampened decorative drawers scattered on the floor. Fumbling, I bend over to collect them as quickly as I can. Crawling around, trying to find my other boot, I hear the door slam, followed by a deep chuckle. I don't hear Reggie's whiny voice, so maybe we're in the clear.

This is not exactly the way I had planned on presenting myself, but sometimes you need to improvise. A look over my shoulder confirms that we are successfully rid of his Celebration Scanner. With the coast confirmed clear, I attempt my sauciest smile before turning and crawling my way over to him, humming a cheery tune.

A wide grin spreads across his ghoulish face and a tremble passes through me at the thought of pleasing him.

"I think you must have forgotten to check your list twice, Santa, because I know I haven't been good enough to have my Christmas wish come true."

He smirks down at me as I continue across the room. His undivided attention feels like too much, and I look down as I get closer.

"Nuh uh uh, my sugar plum, eyes on me."

With his face being so unreadable, it's hard to tell if he is as affected by this as I am. My face flushes as I reach him and sit back on my heels, awaiting my next order. He zeroes in on my cock.

"Never did finish with that, did I?"

Incapable of words at the moment, I just shake my head with a whimper as the gummy worm constricts.

"Let's see if it's in the cards for you." He pulls out a stack of cards. "Or are you more of a dice man?" A pair of dice appears in his hand, which he rolls in a slow circle around his palm suggestively.

Crouching down to get to my level, he whispers in my ear, "You could always give my roulette table another spin?" When I don't answer right away, he leans back, looking at my swollen cock again. "Blow?" he asks.

Another whimper in response.

He laughs maniacally, holding his hand out in front of my face, "The dice, sugar plum! Then we'll find out whether you get lucky tonight."

Good Boy

Sackman

Looking down at the simpering man on his knees at my feet almost has me forfeiting our little game and fucking him right here on the cold stone floor. His whimpers of need are sweeter than any Christmas carol and the glittery spend dripping from his poor neglected cock are almost more than I can bear.

Unfortunately for him, I'm not ready to give up the game just yet. After letting him fester and squirm there for another 45 seconds, I convince myself he's been patient enough that he has earned a little reprieve. We don't have long after all. The big boy has to get back to Christmastown before any of his elves or the pesky Celebration Scanners notice he's gone.

"Have you been good this year? Do you think you deserve to come?" I plaster a sneer on my face to keep up the facade.

"N-n-no I've been very b-bad. But please, I need to come. Please, Sackman." He's so very pretty when he begs.

"Nah ah ah... what do you call me?"

His face falls, but he recovers quickly. "Please, Sack Daddy, may I come?"

Pointing toward the St. Andrew's Cross, no words are needed. My holiday horndog knows where I want him. It may have been an accident that we discovered we both derive pleasure from this type of play, but it isn't something one can easily forget.

Once he's facing the cross, I step up behind him, dragging my palms from his shoulders downward, sweeping off that blasted red coat he's been tempting me with. Goosebumps appear on his ivory skin when the cool air of the lair hits his naked body, the soft thump of the jacket falling to the floor, a note of finality. This is happening, and neither of us wants to stop it.

He remains pliant as I take my sweet time securing first one wrist, then the other, to opposite sides of the cross above his head. Once he's secure, I walk around him, perusing his form and dragging my long, slithering tongue across the back of his neck before standing where he can see me. With a snap, a flogger made of black licorice strands appears in my hand.

"I think," I pause for dramatic effect before I continue. "Twelve lashings will do, don't you, naughty boy?"

He only nods in response, but that won't do.

"Words, my little kinky Kringle. I need your words." My voice is low and demanding as I walk around to his backside. I may be a sadist, but I won't proceed without hearing he's okay with this turn of events.

"Yes, Sack Daddy, I deserve them."

"Good boy." I purr. "Now count them." The last word is punctuated with a light slap of the flogger, the falls barely grazing his upper back.

"One."

Oh, such confidence in his voice now. He's under the misconception I am going to go easy on him when this is really just a warmup. I land another soft blow to his back before moving to the back of his thighs, right under his ass. His cheeks clench at the unexpected change of location and his voice is not quite as strong as he counts now.

"Three."

A low chuckle leaves my lips as I pause before landing hits four and five in quick succession to his juicy sugar plum. The sharp breath he sucks in before counting again has my cock hardening, nearly ready to burst from its sheath.

Six. Seven. Eight. Nine. Ten. By stroke eleven, my blows have gotten hard enough to create a crisp, satisfying sound when they land. The marks left on his body from the licorice falls are a soft red. How festive.

"Eleven!" He shouts, knowing we are close to the end.

Breathing heavily, I waste no time swinging the final blow. Before he can count the last stroke, my body is plastered against his sensitive back and my hand snakes around his hip to his poor, abused cock. My rough palms scratch his shaft as I shuttle my hands up and down his length, providing that little touch of pain that he loves so much alongside his pleasure. He won't last long, and that's the way I like it.

My free hand slides to his throat, squeezing possessively as I release the gummy worm cockring he's had on this entire time. Three more strokes and his cock erupts with his long awaited climax, glittery cum covering my hands as I work him through his orgasm.

Bringing my hand to his mouth, I wipe his own cum across his lips and whisper fondly in his ear.

"Good boy."

Dress Me Up Like a Christmas Tree

Santa

My cock twitches at the praise, gearing up to go again. Licking my lips, the clove and bourbon flavor coats my tongue. Everyone expects my spend to taste like peppermint, but I am far more sophisticated than that. Did I think I would enjoy Sackman forcing me to taste my own cum this much? No. But I'm realizing I'd do just about anything to hear him call me a good boy again. And love every second of it.

He releases my arms from the cross and I all but collapse in front of him, the combined rush of the flogging, delayed release, and praise hitting me at once. This is where I want to be anyway, on my knees, ready to be used in whatever twisted way he can come up with.

A thick hand reaches down, grabbing my beard, forcing me to look up at him.

"My own personal candy cane." His rough hand trails down my back over my tender skin, an involuntary shudder skating through my body.

"You know what I like to do with candy canes?" That long tongue darts out of his mouth, and I suppress a whimper.

He leans in close to my ear. "*Break them,*" he whispers before releasing me to stand to his full height with an evil grin.

Frost, what does it say about me that I want him to break me? I *need* him to break me.

"Please, Sack Daddy." He raises an eyebrow at my begging. "Break me. Use me. Whatever you want. I'm yours."

"That's my arctic penguin," he coos, patting my cheek, before turning and shuffling toward a cabinet on the wall. Without specific instructions, I have no idea what he wants me to do. Stay here? Follow him?

My choice to remain where I am pays off when he glances back over his shoulder, giving me a haunting grin.

"Such an obedient pet." Turning to look through his cabinet, he adds, "You're of no use to me over there, *come.*"

He slaps the side of his sack and I crawl to him like the needy little grub I am. Finding whatever it was he was looking for, he turns to watch me finish my trek across the stone floor.

"Ooh, that's a sight that'll never get old."

Dropping to a crouch in front of me, he shows me what he's got in his hand. Clamps. There's a chain between them and at the end there's a ring. *Fuck.* I just got rid of that damn gummy worm.

Sackman tilts his head to the side and waits, silently asking my permission to continue with this new toy. I nod my head slowly, preparing for what's coming.

One rough hand rubs down my chest, over my belly, toward my glittering cock, which is always ready for him. He slides the cock ring on, stroking me a couple of times just because he can, then pinches a nipple, rolling it between his fingers.

"You're going to look so pretty, all decorated like a Christmas tree."

He finally clamps my nipple, and a hiss escapes unbidden. A nod from me tells him to continue, and he gives my other nipple the same treatment. The chain between my cock and nipples is tightened, so that anytime I move, there's a sharp tug. Moving back to admire his work, he grins like a kid on Christmas morning.

"All we need is a little tinsel and maybe a star." The words feel tangible on my skin as he admires my body at his leisure.

"Or maybe I should baste you in my cum? Add a little Halloween seasoning to this Christmas goose?"

Forgetting my depraved decorations, I attempt to nod eagerly, but even that small movement is enough to tug on the chain and I groan. Sackman's face lights up in delight. He grabs my beard, tilting my chin up high enough that my back arches, the chain completely taut. It's all so much, yet it's not enough.

"Yes," I grunt out.

"Yes, what?" He releases my chin, taking a step back and crossing his arms over his chest.

"Give me your cum, Sack Daddy. Please let me make you feel good."

"You think you deserve my yule log?"

"No," I hedge, walking on my knees toward him. Each step sends a jolt of pain and pleasure through my body. I grab onto his hips. "But you deserve to feel good. If we're not going to be on the nice list, we might as well be really naughty. Use me, Sack Daddy."

"Well, when you put it like that..." His words trail off in an ominous laugh.

His cock stretches from its pouch like a heron's neck and, *fuck*, it's bigger than I remember. In stark contrast to the drab coloring of his body, it's a rainbow of colors. It's ridged, reminding me of one of those long lollipops, except I've never had the urge to have those lollipops jammed down my throat until I can't breathe. My hips thrust involuntarily at the thought of him forcing that lollicock down my throat, which tugs at my clamps yet again. Laughing at my discomfort, he gives himself a slow stroke, a bead of pre-cum forming on the end. Remembering his taste has me licking my lips, needing it more than I've needed anything.

He forcefully grabs my chin, yanking down so my mouth is open and ready for him.

"I'd try not to move, if I were you, or your whole situation might get unpleasant," he says, as he shoves his rainbow shaft into my mouth. The assault starts slow as he holds my head back, keeping my clamps tight while he drags his cock from my mouth, leaving just the tip inside. I swirl my tongue and suck hard, my cheeks hollowing, as I finally get the taste I've been craving for so long. Sweet and smoky, like the best spiced cider.

I've searched the world for something as good, but nothing comes close to his special sauce.

I grab his hips, trying to pull him closer to show him I can take more, but he pulls away completely, tugging my head back even further in response.

"You're not in charge here, red. Remember that." A curt reminder before he pushes his dick back in my mouth and I relax, letting him thoroughly fuck my face. The onslaught makes my eyes water as I gag on him, but he doesn't stop.

"That's my Christmas cum slut. You needed this cock, didn't you?"

"Mhm," a grunt around his rainbow rod is all I can manage. He continues pounding my face and my grip on his hips is my only lifeline.

Suddenly, he pulls out of my mouth, grabs my hand from its position on his hip and uses it to stroke himself to completion, coming all over my face and chest. His gaze turns reverent as he looks down at me, covered in his cum, my cock throbbing, nipples aching, as if I'm a work of art. And fuck if I don't feel like it. Not wanting to break this connection, I simply lean forward and lick his cock clean while staring into the void of his eyes.

He runs his hands through my hair, the roughness sending tingles throughout my body.

"You look better than any fancy Christmas decoration right now, snowflake."

Here Comes Santa Claus

Sackman

A primal groan leaves Santa's lips as my praise washes over him, making him shudder. Most people look at me and think I am the epitome of all things wicked, scary, and vile. I mean, they're not wrong, but something about giving this holiday heathen what he truly craves causes a sweet heat to bloom from my chest.

Much like that green hairy fucker up on that mountain, I don't have a heart, so in actuality, it's probably just heartburn or something.

As much of an asshole as I am, I won't leave my Christmas cutie unsatisfied. He's been so very good, and obedience deserves a reward.

Leaning down, I remove the clamps from his nipples one at a time, a hiss leaving his mouth as I lave the sensitive peaks to soothe them with my dexterous tongue. In juxtaposition to the rough treatment I just gave him, gentle hands slide the metal ring from his shaft. The poor thing has really been abused today.

My palm settles beneath his chin before applying firm upward pressure, encouraging him to stand without words. Once on his feet, my grip moves to his limp palm, dragging him behind me to the mound of blankets and pillows in the back corner of my lair.

I've always had this here, but the red velvet fabric is a new addition since Santa left my embrace last year. The soft fabric matches the color of his suit perfectly, and no one but us knows its significance. If we want to keep it that way, we are going to need to speed up our little tryst more than I'd like. I could keep playing with his jack-o'-lantern all night long, offering up tricks and treats in succession to keep him on his boot-clad toes. Alas, some things will just have to wait until next year.

A gentle push urges my charge down on the makeshift bed, my plush body following behind him. Ice-blue eyes never leave mine as the big man submits fully to me, spreading his luscious body beneath me as if in offering to a higher power. He may be the sacrifice, but I'm the one who will be worshiping at his altar this time.

Sliding my palms up his body, I squeeze the back of his neck gently but with possessiveness, communicating without words the care I harbor for him deep down. My eyes never leave his as my voice ekes out in a rasp.

"On your hands and knees."

Tearing my gaze away, I help him turn over to his bowl full of jelly, gripping his hips once he's prone to lift them where I want them. Heavy breaths tear out of both of us as I grip the cheeks of his sugar plum ass and spread them, getting an eyeful of his tight hole, puckered like lips after eating a particularly sour candy.

A groan leaves my chest before I spit straight onto the bud, his cheeks clenching under my palms when it makes contact.

"P-please."

The stuttered plea from his supple lips is what finally snaps my spider-web thin control. Lining up my lollicock with his entrance, my hips gently push forward as my tip breaches his snowy cave. To my surprise, there isn't much resistance and a sinister thought hits me.

"Oh, snowflake, have you been stretching this icy asshole for me? Thinking about how full my thick candy dick makes you feel?" I rub a soothing palm down his spine as I coo at him, sinking another three inches into his tight channel.

"Yes!" It's more of a ragged cry than a word, but I understand it all the same.

A sigh escapes me when I am finally fully seated inside jolly old St. Nick, my hips flush with the round globes of his ass. Wasting no time, I pull out swiftly before slamming back in again to the hilt, repeating the motion again, and again, and again, until the pounding I am gifting him becomes so rough he struggles to stay upright.

My hand slides back up his spine until I can get a grip on the silvery strands of his hair, yanking back until he is upright on his knees, his back plastered to my front tighter than a slutty latex cat Halloween costume. One hand remains secure on his hip while the other slides around, down his jolly jawline until resting on his throat. The sounds of our lovemaking echo through the cavern, loud and lascivious enough I would be surprised if all nine of his reindeer couldn't hear us from here.

"Fuuuck, Santa baby, you feel better than taking the whole bowl of candy when the sign says to only take one." I'm not going to last long, it's too good. But he needs to come before me, because I am nothing if not a gentleman. The hand on his hip glides forward to wrap around his candy cane-hard cock, stroking in time with my frantic thrusts to bring us both over the edge. His length swells in my palm, his baubles draw up tight to his body, and I know he's almost there.

Leaning forward, I trace a line up to the spot just below his ear with my tongue, following with my hot breath on his skin.

"Here comes Santa Claus."

My whisper is drawled out and punctuated with a nip to his earlobe, pushing him over the edge, screaming my name as his hot glittery cum coats my hand and the plush red velvet beneath us. His pleasure, along with the tightening around my candy cock, sets me off too, and I fill Santa's sack with my own kind of present, not stopping until he's milked every last drop from me.

Breathing hard, we slowly come down from our high, and as I gain back the ability to speak, I can't help one last growl to my perfect paramour.

"You won't need any of those treats left out for you this year with my milk in your cookie. Too bad no one will know that's what you truly want for Christmas."

X-rated Reindeer Games

Santa

S ackman doesn't release me right away, allowing me to relish the feeling of his arms wrapped around me like a snug Christmas ribbon. His hand on my neck grips me possessively, and I almost confess my true Christmas wish.

I'd give up all the milk and cookies in the world for more time with him.

He drags his hand down my body to my hip as he slowly pulls his enormous member out from my merry maker. Not quite ready for our contact to end, I place my hands over his to hold him to me. I'm needed back in Christmastown, but a few more moments of selfishness can't possibly cause that much damage, right? Flashbacks to the mayhem of last Christmas cross my mind. Today's not Christmas. The town will survive without me for a little longer.

With the x-rated reindeer games finished, I'm left raw and open, suddenly fully aware of my vulnerable position. There's no one I trust more to give me everything that I crave physically, to know just how to completely wreck me in the best possible way, but without knowing he returns my feelings, can I trust that he won't also destroy my heart?

"Come on, my little tinsel tart, let's get you cleaned up." He slides an arm behind my knees, the other going behind my neck to scoop me up as if I'm no heavier than a fluffy snowball. Instinctively, I curl into his rough chest as he carries me into the bathroom.

Like everything in his lair, it's large and moody. The complete opposite of my bright cheery cottage. In place of the bright twinkle lights I have draped all about my rooms, he has flickering candles which cast an eerie glow.

He gently places me on the seat in his cavernous shower, plenty large enough for the both of us, as he gets the water to the right temperature. The water beads on his fabric, somehow not soaking him through. When he's happy with the heat, he reaches a hand out to me, pulling me up to stand.

With the same level of intensity he used to torture me, he treasures me, taking his time to rinse off my entire body before he spins me in his arms to wet my hair. For a nightmare man with no need for such things, I can't help but notice the amount of hair products he has in his shower. An Arctic Narwhal shampoo bottle sits next to a peppermint bark beard oil, suspiciously all the same brands I use back at the North Pole.

Taking his time, he lathers my hair with shampoo, using his rough hands to scratch and massage my scalp. The same care is taken with my beard, holding me close to his chest as he washes and oils it. So slowly, he moves on to wash my entire body, his burlap hands exfoliating my skin, turning it as red as my coat. When he's satisfied with a job well done, he gently pushes me toward the seat, dropping to his knees in front of me.

Maintaining eye contact, he slides his snake tongue along my length. Despite everything we've been through today, the sight of him on his knees in front of me has me lighting up like Rudolph's nose. His tongue curls completely around my shaft, a wicked grin remaining on his face as he pleasures me. It's so much better than I remember, my hand and imagination have not been doing him justice.

"Be a good boy now Santa baby and give me one more," he growls before taking my cinnamon stick completely into his gaping mouth. He pulls back, swirling that tongue around me, looking like a colorful stripe on my candy cane. I drop my head back against the shower wall.

Licking me from base to tip like his favorite dessert, he says, "That's my polar bear. You need your big, bad Sack Daddy to make you come, don't you?"

Taking me fully into his mouth again, his head bobs up and down and I grab onto the tip of his sack, moaning my agreement. He has no idea how true that is. How his is the only face I picture when I'm tugging my reins. How nothing else fills me the way his lollicock does. He has no idea that I've become reliant on my elves reporting any behavior at the North Pole because I can't stop watching him through my portal viewer.

I watch him while he sleeps. I watch him while he's awake. I know how it feels when he's bad, and I love that he's not good, for goodness' sake.

I'm jerked back to the moment when he rolls my balls in one hand like a pair of jingle bells while his tongue plays with the tip of my cock, dipping in and out of the slit before wrapping back around the head. The scratching sensation of his rough palms stroking my length is almost too much. When I whimper, he chuckles.

"Don't worry, my jolly giant, I'm done playing games with my sweet toy, wouldn't want to break it."

When Sackman calls me his, it pushes me over.

"Mmff - my christmas tree is about to be flocked," I moan out seconds before exploding down his throat. Sackman takes every shimmering drop, his swallow constricting around my cock as he does.

Once he's sucked me dry, he stands, looming over me, and says with a grin, "I do so love it when Santa comes down my chimney."

I reach out for his sack, ready to coax his cock out again and return the favor, but he stops me with a squeeze of my hand, before spinning away from me to turn off the water. He quickly reaches out of the shower and grabs a fluffy red towel, wrapping me in it and carrying me back to his nest of blankets–which have somehow been cleaned. Too tired to ask how, I let him remove the towel and tuck me into bed, scooting behind me and wrapping a large arm around my nude form. He nuzzles into my shoulder, his warm breath tickling my neck.

"Sleep tight, Christmas cookie."

I guess I shouldn't be surprised that a guy stuffed with candy is as sweet as he is, but it's a side of him so few get to see.

Just as I'm about to drift off, visions of sugar-plums beginning their dance in my head, the door slams open and I hear Reginald's panicked voice.

"So sorry to interrupt, Mr. Sackman, but this really can't wait."

His voice raises an octave as he squeaks, "Santa, is that you?"

Randy? Reggie? Roger? Whatever

Sackman

I t takes everything in me not to release a feral growl when that sniveling tattle tale barges into my chambers uninvited and unexpected. Instinctively my body wrenches to a sitting position, shifting to protect my naked lover from prying eyes. That view is for my eye-voids and my eye-voids alone.

"What the fuck are you doing here, Randy?" I bellow, my anger palpable as it echoes off the walls of the cavern.

The twit has the gall to try to correct me. "It's R-r-r... Reginald, sir."

"I don't give a quilted bitch's asshole what it is! Get. OUT!"

Reginald practically vibrates with fear, but he stands his ground. My heart is pounding like reindeer hooves on a snowy roof because if this mofo goes back to the Occasion Official and rats us out, all hell will break loose. There would be magical barriers put in place, extra Celebration Scanners assigned to both of us all year long. Sure, last year was a true kidnapping, but they don't know that Nicky here came–pfft... *came*–willingly this year. Oh so very willingly.

Our clandestine trysts need to stay just that: hidden away like those eggs that pesky rabbit stashes in the spring. The more I think about it, though, the tighter my chest gets with frustration. Why should they look down on us for this? Obviously we are opposites. Light versus dark, sweet versus sour. But opposites attract don't they? From the outside, our activities may look aggressive and evil, but it comes from a deep place of care and trust, completely consensual.

I may act hard, but I am completely soft for Santa.

Reggie hasn't moved during my entire 45 second inner monologue, so I close my eyes, take a deep breath to calm myself, then look back at him.

"What is so important that you had to invade my personal space, Roger?"

He doesn't correct me this time, just forges on with a sputtering cadence.

"The Occasion Official is on their way!"

That lights a fire under my fabric ass. "What?!"

"Santa didn't come back from the meeting," Reginald pauses to look pointedly at the man himself before continuing. "Everyone was looking for him, dashing through the snow because they were worried when he didn't arrive in Christmastown. Hazel made a report to the board, and, after last year's debacle, the OO decided to come here themself in case you...uh...non-consensually took Santa on a trip again."

The words that were tumbling from Reggie's mouth like needles from a Christmas tree in February finally cease, giving way to silence as we all process that information. The little man's gaze bounces rapidly from me to Santa and back, and my skin bristles in anticipation of his judgment. He must see the challenge in my eyes because before I can formulate a response, he sweeps his hand in the air as if brushing away cobwebs.

"Oh no, I don't care about that. About, uh, your *relationship*. But I'm not sure that the Occasion Official will be so understanding. I came here to warn you they were coming because if you *had* taken Santa on an impromptu vacation, things would get messy."

"Fudge! Galloping gum drop son of a snowman! What do we do?" Santa's frantic voice finally joins the fray as I reach for him, needing to touch him to ground us both.

As much as I'd like to shout our pairing from the spires of that pumpkin prick's castle and beyond, it isn't the right time. Surprisingly, it's Reginald who jumps in with a solution. His expression softens slightly as he looks at my balsam beau.

"Hazel is outside with your sleigh. You can pretend you were here to deliver Sackman his yearly coal, then you can dash away, dash away, dash away with all your reindeer back to Christmastown, the OO being none the wiser."

Huh. That's actually a pretty good idea. But why...

"Why are you helping us?" Santa voices the thought I was just completing in my head.

Reggie's cheeks flush cherry red as he tucks his chin and looks at anything but us. Ah, I know what this is.

"You like Hazel, don't you, Reggie boy?"

Reggie's eyes snap up in surprise that I got his name correct, then he slowly dips his head to confirm.

"I think we may be able to put in a good word, maybe even set up a little investigative trip for you both where the cabin only has one bed and, oops! I guess you will have to share. Can't we, sugar?" Hope shines in Reginald's eyes as Santa nods his agreement.

His voice is more confident, albeit a bit forlorn as he tells the timid Celebration Scanner, "Stall them for a few minutes Reggie. I'll be out to my sleigh post haste."

The small man nods, spinning on his heels in a rush to do Santa's bidding, when I stop him with a hand on his arm. Mustering all the earnestness I possess, I squeeze his shoulder.

"Thank you."

More flushed cheeks and a small nod are all he manages before he speeds away. I look back at my lover, disappointed to see he's already dressed, fully wrapped in his red suit with the black buckle done up tight and the tufted hat covering his silky silver strands of hair.

"One day." I say to him longingly in anticipation of when we can spend more than a single moment a year together.

"One day." He echoes back to me sadly before bringing that gloved hand back to his face and tapping his nose, an ironic callback to hours ago when he used the same magic to bring himself here to me. Only this time, when he disappears in a whirl of sparkles, he leaves the cave–and my soul– feeling bereft.

Saved by the TEAMS Chime

Santa

When I apparate into my sleigh, Hazel doesn't even look up from whatever she's doing on her phone.

"Nick, if you wanted to go trick or treating, you should've said something." She's holding back a smile.

With a grunt and flick of my wrists, we're immediately on our way back to Christmastown. The farther away I get from Sackman, the more I feel like I'm making a mistake. I can still see him at the quarterly Seasonal Symposiums. That will have to suffice. Plus, I can always check in on him when I'm making my naughty and nice list. That counts as official business.

Who knows? Maybe this year, I won't catch him doing something naughty. Or maybe he *will* be doing something very naughty, knowing I'm watching. Something just for me.

I shake my head, refocusing on the sleigh, even though my reindeer could make the flight on autopilot. If he wanted more out of this, he would've asked for it. He's a sack who has no problem taking what he wants. I have no doubt he'd threaten the OO to get what he desired. I can learn to survive with only my glimpses of him, my fantasies, and my hand. Our one day a year will have to be enough.

Spinkletark rushes me the second we land. "Oh Santa, we were worried sick about you!"

I smile and greet my elves, going through the motions as expected, but my heart's not in it. I left that back in Halloweenville.

Hazel, noticing my apathetic mood, shoos the elves away. "Let's give Santa some space. It looks like he could use a rest."

To me, she says quietly, "Listen Nick, I'm not going to pretend to understand your arrangement, but helping out Santa seems like the best way for me to stay on the nice list. So understand I have your best interests at heart when I tell you to quit acting like you've been banished to the island of misfit toys and start acting like the boss leather daddy I know you are."

She shrugs and walks away, returning her attention to her phone.

Maybe we had the wrong idea about these Celebration Scanners.

I've made it through a quarter of the year without seeing my special sack in person. Sure, I watch him daily and think of him nightly, but it's not the same. Hazel is fully aware of my intentions to see Sackman today after the symposium. Hopefully, we can get some alone time without setting off an interseasonal crisis.

Per our agreement, Hazel is going to work with Reggie to secure some kind of recurring opportunity, I just need to make sure that it's what my beast of a bag wants. I haven't seen him use anyone else to satisfy his needs. And trust me, I've been watching. When that beautiful cock comes out and he strokes himself, I can't help but follow along, matching his every movement.

I'm ready to frost my cookie right here in my pants at just the thought of him, so when he walks into the room, I can't help but bite my lip, holding in a whimper. A corner of his mouth kicks up, witnessing my obvious discomfort, and there's a little more swagger in his step as he takes the seat directly across from me. I'm considering saying fuck it all and crawling under this table to beg for his candy.

Sackman: You're drooling, Claus.

Saved by the TEAMS chime. Licking my lips, I stare him down.

Sackman: I've missed those lips, snowflake. Red and shiny, like a candied apple.

A blush creeps up my cheeks. I don't stand a chance against him and he knows it.

Santa: What else did you miss?

Sackman: You. Ass up. In my bed.

I gasp, then choke, then try to play it off as a cough. All eyes turn to me as my face goes completely red. Grabbing a glass for some water in an attempt to play it cool, Sackman's low chuckle goes straight to my cock.

Sackman: Want to play a game, Nicky?

Santa: No

The OO looks expectantly at me and I realize they must have asked me a question.

"I'm sorry, could you repeat that?"

Sackman: No more playtime?

Santa: No more games.

In an irritated tone, the OO repeats, "I said, how are things going with the Celebration Scanners? I assume there have been no more interruptions to your work in Christmastown? No *incidents* with other seasonal representatives?"

Sackman: What are you saying, Claus?

I scoff. "Ms. Cracklebottom is doing a fine job, certainly. But I am concerned that this additional overhead is a waste of resources. Entirely unnecessary."

The OO crosses their arms. "You realize this oversight was put into place for *your* protection, Santa?"

Something snaps inside me, like a pine branch weighed down by too much ice.

"We are grown adults and should be able to speak with whomever we please without concern about how it will affect our holidays." I sit up straighter in my chair, channeling the stern leather daddy energy Hazel mentioned into my voice. "Frankly, if I want to speak with Mr. Sackman after 'the incident', I should be able to without having Hazel read and approve each message."

"What exactly would you need to say to the Halloween representative, Mr. Claus?" the OO asks in a terse tone.

"Yes, Santa, what would you want to say to me?" Sackman grins as he poses his question.

"I, uh," I fumble, confidence flickering, trying to find the words. I know what I want to say, but now's not the time and the middle of the quarterly Seasonal Symposium is not the place.

"You know what? Fuck it. I'm obsessed with you. I can't stop thinking about you. I watch you all the time to see the naughty things you do and I fucking love all of them. I fucking love *you*. That's what I wanted to say to you, you big sack, alright?"

With that pronouncement, I jump over the table and throw myself into his lap as cries of outrage fill the room.

Sack Daddy Approves

Sackman

It's a good thing I am a literal sack filled with soft candy because when Santa launches himself at me, the big man has so much momentum he knocks me backward, tipping the chair until we land on the hard linoleum floor, a soft "oof" escaping my lips.

Chaos is erupting around us. Gasps from Spinkletark and that Tina Toothfairy prude, clutching their imaginary pearls as they realize what's happening. A chorus of "awws" and "whoops" from the group of pagans representing Beltane over by the Occasion Official's podium. Shouts from said Occasion Official as they bang their gavel to get everyone to settle down. I didn't even know that fuck had a gavel.

Awareness of my surroundings flees my concern just as quickly as it arrived, my focus zeroing in on my secret lover. Well, not-so-secret anymore, I suppose. Santa hasn't moved, the warm weight of him a comfort as he presses his velvet-clad body to mine.

We are such opposites. My villainous nature to his giving one. My scratchy skin to his plush red coat. My dominance to his submission. By all the books, we shouldn't work, but as I said earlier, opposites attract right?

In the end, the opinions of others mean nothing to me if those shiny blue eyes keep looking at me in adoration and vulnerability as they are right now. If loving him is wrong, I don't want to be right.

Staring back at him, I try to portray my determination through my gaze, willing him to understand now that he's gone rogue and spilled the jellybeans about our relationship, I am never letting him go. One hand slides to the back of his alabaster neck, the other gripping his snowdrift soft hip as I swiftly flip our positions, trapping the breathless man beneath me.

"Oh, Santa baby, how very naughty of you to cause such a scene here." I purr the words as a sinister smile tips up the corners of my lips. "But also so very brave. Sack Daddy approves."

His body loosens beneath me, my praise eradicating any anxiety he may have had from his daring leap of faith. Can't let that last too long.

Leaning forward, my tongue snakes out to lick a sweet stripe along the line of his jaw until I'm close enough to whisper in his ear, ensuring this part is kept between just the two of us.

"That doesn't mean I won't roast your chestnuts later, though."

Satisfaction rolls through me when I'm rewarded with his hips thrusting up, his hard cock ready to burst from his velvet seam before my lips crash to his in a painful dance of passion.

The rest of the world can fuck off for all I care. Old St Nick spends his life spoiling brats around the world. Now it's my turn to spoil him for as long as he'll have me.

Epilogue

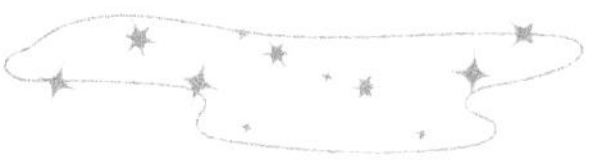

Santa

"That's it, snowflake." Sackman's rough voice still sends chills down my spine, even after all this time. "Look at you taking my cock like the filthy frosty you are." He shoves his cock fully down my throat, cutting off my air supply for a moment, before pulling back and letting me catch my breath.

"What would your elves think if they came out here and saw how bad you want this, Nicky?" I moan around his cock as he slowly thrusts in and out of my mouth.

My devious darling surprised me at work, quickly using my reins to restrain me as he has his way with me in my sleigh. Sackman is working his way through my life, christening anything and everything he can, marking me fully as his.

He pulls himself from my mouth with a grunt. "I need to fill your snowglobe," he growls, lifting me up and flipping me over. Chuckling, he tugs down my pants, leaving me bent over my sleigh, completely exposed. He leans over me, stroking my cock as he whispers in my ear, "Are you ready for me, big boy?"

"Always," I moan out, already so close. When he's not actively fucking me, I'm prepping for him to fuck me, my life revolving around him like a toy train around a Christmas tree.

"Such a good boy," he says with a chuckle, pushing into me and wrapping that sinfully scratchy hand around my cock. He continues stroking me and fucking me until I've made a complete mess of the sleigh. He follows shortly after, filling me with his cum. Sackman reaches out, smearing my release all over the sleigh, making it sparkle, before putting his hand in my mouth for me to clean.

"Messy, messy, messy," he chides as he pulls out of me and slaps my rump then spins me around to tug up my pants.

"Don't forget who you belong to, Claus."

I barely resist rolling my eyes, pulling him into a hard kiss instead, his prehensile tongue snaking around my mouth. If his love language is having his cum drip out of my ass to thoroughly mark me as his, I'll take it. I'll take him in whatever form he wants to give me.

Reluctantly breaking our kiss, I pull back and squeeze his sides.

"Spinkletark needed to speak with me about... actually, I'm not sure, I wasn't listening. I can make it quick and then maybe we can grab a bite to eat or something?" I raise an eyebrow.

"Or something," he grumbles, noncommittally.

I give a quick glance to the sleigh. Hopefully, cum isn't too hard to wash out, though at least it's festive. We leave the stable and start walking to the workshop. I'm not sure where Spinkletark is, but they're usually in one of the workrooms this time of day.

We run into a few other elves without any sign of Spinkletark. I'm about to give up and try to meet with him tomorrow, when I hear muffled noises coming from behind a closed door. I slide open the door and stifle a gasp. My beastly beau chuckles darkly behind me, and I elbow him in the gut.

"It's not what it looks like!" Spinkletark yells from where they are strapped to a makeshift spanking bench. The woodworker in me wants to examine it more closely. Every other part of me decides I don't need a closer look at Spinkletark's tree trimmings. They tug against their restraints, but they are not budging. Somehow, their ass is even redder than their face. Didn't know the little elf had it in them.

"Mmmf," Reggie adds, an ornament stuffed in his mouth like a gag. He's strapped to one of our wrapping stations, the ribbon usually reserved for good little boys and girls being repurposed. I hold in a chuckle at the bow tied neatly around his cock. I bet he can't wait for someone to unwrap that present, if the pre-cum dripping down his shaft is any indication.

"It's exactly what it looks like," Hazel says, standing on the table over Reggie, one sinful black stiletto pressed into his chest. He whimpers beneath her.

She's taken the sexy librarian vibe to a whole new level. If I didn't already have my own Sack Daddy possessively gripping me, I wouldn't mind her punishing me for being too loud.

Looking between Spinkletark and Reggie, I'm guessing she's making these boys real loud today.

"But we're all consenting adults, so if you don't mind." She waves her hand to the door. "Get in or get out."

Bonus Epilogue
Occasion Official

There is nothing I love more than the satisfaction of completing another form flawlessly. The loops and swirls as I sign my name with a regal flourish make my chest tight with satisfaction as I sit back, admiring another job well done. The only benefit of managing a bunch of holiday hooligans is that it is my official duty to fill out all this glorious paperwork when they inevitably make a mess of things.

The door swings open behind me and I deliberately place the cap on my limited edition Magic Majuscules fountain pen, aligning the rose gold accents with precision. I certainly would not want the ink to dry out, damaging the delicate nib, while I'm dealing with one of said buffoons.

"Hello, Ms. Toothfairy. You're early," I say when I don't hear the padding of footsteps after the door clicks shut.

"I just need a moment of your time, OO." Her voice is nothing more than a tinkle floating to my ears upon the light breeze caused by her gossamer wings.

Tina flutters over to the table beside me, resting her plump ass next to my stack of completed forms. Her wings flit nervously and the papers beside her rustle. That would be all I need right now. My chest is now tight for a different reason. The possibility of seeing my forms scattered on the floor, covered in sparkly fairy dust, is squeezing my heart with anxiety. That despicable stuff never comes off completely.

I suppose I am not as discreet as I had hoped because she notices me eyeing the forms, and stands, straightening her obnoxiously short skirt.

"What was it that you needed, Ms. Toothfairy? The other *real* holiday representatives should be arriving shortly. I do not have an excess of time to dedicate to other pseudo-holiday creatures." I force a roughness into my tone, but as she takes the seat next to me, crossing her legs, exposing just a hint too much, it's getting harder for me to pretend I'm not affected.

She twirls a strand of chestnut hair around her finger, playing up an innocent look.

"Please OO, I've told you. Call me Tina." She places her hand on my forearm, the contact sending a jolt of desire through me, even before her next words.

"I can't help but notice you've been so stressed lately. There's got to be *something* I can do to help take a load off of your plate. Want me to review these for you?"

The words are soaked in innuendo, subtlety has flown out the window, much like she did the last time we were intimate. She floats up and over my desk until she is hovering directly in front of me, placing her hands on the table and perusing the agenda for today's meeting. Looking over her shoulder, she tugs her lush bottom lip between her teeth, angling her hips up even further before she continues.

"Shall I double check the minutes from the last meeting? Make sure you didn't miss anything?"

If she wasn't so tempting I may have taken offense at her comment that I may have missed something, but the only action I can manage now is to swallow and nod, taking in the gorgeous view she's giving me. From where I am seated, it's obvious she's not wearing a damn thing under that tiny skirt. We both know full well her goody two shoes exterior is just an act, but someone could walk into the conference room at any moment.

"Tina," I whisper.

"Hmm," she replies lazily, feigning intense focus on my papers.

"It seems you're the one who has missed something, Tina." I trail my hands up her thighs, reveling in the feel of her soft umber skin as I spread her cheeks open, exposing her dripping wet pussy. Pressing my thumb into her without preamble, I urge her to continue.

"The meeting minutes, Tina."

"The Occasion Official hereinafter referred to as O-Ohhh," she begins, my name being drawn out into moans as I plunge my face forward, driving my tongue into her slit.

"Why did you stop, Tina? Notice a clerical error already?" Oh, how I love to tease her in this way.

"No, OO, sorry," she replies, voice breathy. "Um, the OO called the meeting to order." She continues through the minutes as I continue devouring her pussy. She tastes just as sweet as I remember, needing her flavor on my tongue is a vice I could easily develop.

"When asked about the Celebration Scanners, the Christmas Representative stated... nngh.. stated that they were satisfactory however may be a waste of resources before professing his love for the Halloween Representative, throwing himself across the room causing damage to furniture as well as ho... ah... holiday issued equipment including but not limited to computers, tablets, and a stocked fruit and vegetable cornucopia."

Remembering all of the delicious forms I was able to fill out following that little incident, my pace quickens, my tongue battering her clit as my arousal grows. The paperwork took me absolutely *hours*. Father Time! I'm close to coming right now at just the thought of it.

Of course, I'd much rather see her fall apart first, and I know just the thing to push her over the finish line faster. Reaching to the table beside me, I wrap my fingers around my gavel, twirling it in my hands before trailing the end through her wetness. Those needy hips push back, searching for more. If we had more time, I would make sure she was a simpering mess before giving her the penetration she craves, but alas the meeting will start soon, and I absolutely abhor being late.

With one hand spreading her open, I slowly insert the intricately carved handle into her warm, pink cunt. Standing to loom over her, I continue thrusting the gavel in and out of Tina while yanking her top down so that I can play with her ample breasts.

"That's it, my filthy little fairy. You're going to come on my gavel like the slutty sprite you are." Peaking quickly, she cries out, fairy dust filling the air around us. I remove my gavel from her glitter box and toss it onto my podium, then flip my little fairy around, looking her sternly in the eyes.

"Thank you for your assistance reviewing the minutes, my hovering harlot. You're going to need to fix yourself up quickly so you don't look so thoroughly fucked when the others arrive."

"Of course, OO, only one thing first," she says between heaving breaths. "Hands on the table."

Curious where this may lead, I obey. She pulls my robes up my body, displaying what I put on this morning, hoping she'd find it. A cute pink corset and matching lace thong.

"Is this for me? You know I adore pink." She snaps the thong with a giggle. Pulling the lace to the side, she pushes something cold into my ass. She gives my butt cheek a slap before dropping my robes back into place. "Be a good OO and keep that in for the whole meeting, understood?" I shrug. It's not like I could pull a plug out discreetly, anyway.

Tina readjusts herself, smoothing her skirt and pulling up her top as I compile my papers, grab my gavel, and move to the head of the room. Any idiot could tell what has just occurred here given the obscene amount of fairy dust, but luckily the holiday representatives are too self absorbed to notice even the most obvious details.

The holiday representatives file in over the next 45 seconds, and at precisely 8:00, I enthusiastically grab my gavel with a smirk, thinking of where it last was. I am about to raise it, prepared to call the meeting to attention, when I freeze. A shiver runs up my spine from my ass, where the plug has started buzzing. My eyes snap to Tina, who is sitting in the front row, typing away on her computer, not a care in the world. Until I notice a small pink controller sitting to the side of her hand. She'll be paying for that later.

Looking around the room, I chuckle to myself that we thought we could control these heathens. Santa is currently staring at the Halloween representative as if he wants to crawl inside his sack. The pathetic Springtime Snail is standing right outside the window, sadly holding his "Make Springtime Slimy Again" sign up for all to see. And my pretty pixie is subtly licking her lips and spreading her legs, giving me another glimpse of her fairy ring.

Banging my gavel on my podium, I announce, "I call this," not-so-boring, "meeting to order."

About Unfortunate Reads

Cassie is an ADHD millennial mom of one from Baltimore who loves craft beer and chaos. Though she runs the Unfortunate Reads page, she reads and enjoys more than just the absolutely unhinged stories. She likes her books extra spicy, with a special fondness for PNR, Sci/fi, and Why Choose romance.

Cassie is a sex positive, feminist, LGBTQIA+ ally who supports indie authors and human artists. She loves to interact with the bookstagram/booktok communities. There is no room for disparagement of books, authors, or readers on her pages. **Reading is reading!**

She began publishing in 2024, and quickly caught the writing bug. She is also a narrator, cover designer, and generally can't pick one facet of the book world to stay in which is how she started running the Monsterotica Book Con.

You can find her online at:

Instagram: @unfortunate.reads

TikTok: @unfortunatereads

unfortunatereads.com

Cassie's Other Works
(under various pseudonyms)

Writing:

The Time of Her Life

Handle Me

Pushin' Cushions (cowritten with Vera Valentine)

Narration:

As Unfortunate Reads:

Stiff by Thea Masen, (Duet narration with Richard Pendrag-
on)

As Aspen Destrier:

The Fire Goddess by Amber Collins

Whatever Works by Amber Collins

The Shrinking App by Amber Collins

The Wellington Ruse by Sarah Welk Baynum

About Nicole Parker

Nicole Parker is an AuDHD, 30-something California native who spends the great majority of her free time writing books, reading books, or organizing her ever growing TBR list. She also has a spouse, some kids, and pets, but this isn't about them.

She began publishing in 2024 after quickly falling in love with the sentient object romance world. She took the concept of "there are no bad ideas" to heart and really ran with it.

You can find her online at booksbynicoleparker.com

Also by Nicole Parker

The Kyleverse Series

Weird things happen to the people around Kyle, but his go with the flow, try anything once attitude usually leads to a good time.

The Kyleverse is a series of sentient object romance short stories. Kyle isn't the main character, but he shows up to help the plot in one way or another. The stories are sequential but can be read as standalones.

Fully Charged

(cowritten with Unfortunate Reads)

Jewel is a newly single mom who just wants to unwind in her rare time alone. The kids are away, and it's time for mama to play...with herself. Except the off-brand batteries in her favorite tool die mid-session. When she replaces them with the industry leader, Ohm-azing, Jewel gets more than long lasting pleasure.

Wattson has been sent from Ohm-azing headquarters to ensure Jewel is 100% satisfied.

Fully Charged is a parody sentient object romance intended for audiences over 18 years old. This contains intimate relations between a human woman and a mythical pink rabbit.

Any Amazon affiliate links on these pages earn Unfortunate Reads a ***very*** *(I mean very)* small commission. Amazon makes me tell you, so...click at your own risk?

www.ingramcontent.com/pod-product-compliance
Lightning Source LLC
Chambersburg PA
CBHW060338310726
48976CB00007B/2606